Slasher

by Allison Moore

A SAMUEL FRENCH ACTING EDITION

FOUNDED 1830

NEW YORK HOLLYWOOD LONDON TORONTO

SAMUELFRENCH.COM

ISBN 978-0-573-69861-3   Printed in U.S.A.   #29140

MUSIC USE NOTE

IMPORTANT BILLING AND CREDIT REQUIREMENTS

SLASHER was first produced at the 2009 Humana Festival of New American Plays at Actors Theater of Louisville on March 6, 2009. The production was directed by Josh Hecht, with scenic design by Paul Owen, costume design by Jennifer Caprio, lighting design by Russell Champa, sound designer by Matt Callahan, properties design by Doc Manning, dialect coaching by Rinda Frye, and fight direction by K. Jenny Jones. The production stage manager was Robin Grady, the production assistant was Melissa Blair, and the dramaturg was Amy Wegener. Casting by Alaine Alldaffer Casting. The cast was as follows:

FRANCES MCKINNEY . . . . Lusia Strus

CHRISTI GRACI AND OTHERS . . . . Christy McIntosh

MARC HUNTER . . . . Mark Setlock

SHEENA MCKINNEY . . . . Nicole Rodenburg

HILDY MCKINNEY . . . . Katharine Moeller

JODY JOSHI . . . . Lucas Papaelias

CHARACTERS

SHEENA MCKINNEY – 21, girl-next-door kind of pretty. Not book-smart, but a survivor.

HILDY MCKINNEY – 15, Sheena's little sister. Smarter than Sheena, but less capable in a crisis.

FRANCES MCKINNEY – 40-50, their mother. Angry, thwarted feminist with a questionable disability. Gets around her house with the aid of a li'l rascal scooter. Loud.

MARC HUNTER – 35-40, a D-list director and recovering alcoholic and sex addict. Tells everyone he's younger than he is.

JODY JOSHI – 23, an undergrad film school dude. Capable, knows his stuff, but kind of a kiss-ass.

CHRISTI GARCIA – 23-30, Assistant Director of the Holy Shepherd Justice League. Very put together, as if she's always ready to make a statement on camera. Not to be underestimated.

BRIDGET/MARCY/BETH/MADISON – attractive young women who are killed in various ways, all to be played by the actor playing CHRISTI GARCIA.

WOMAN/CAR HOP/RADIO ANNOUNCER/NEWS ANCHOR – also to be played/voiced by the actor playing CHRISTI GARCIA

SETTING

In and around Austin, Texas, 2007. Frances' run down house; a Hooter's-style bar; a Sonic drive in; another house where they film.

AUTHOR'S NOTE

As the play progresses, Sheena's life begins to resemble a horror movie; acting and production choices should reflect this.

PROLOGUE

(Flash back, 1992. The construction site. Darkness. Night. Sound of rain.)

WOMAN'S VOICE. No...no, please...

(A crack of thunder, and a flash of lightening reveals **FRANCES,** *searching for the source of the voice.)*

(Another flash of lightening, and we see two shadowy **FIGURES** – *a* **WOMAN** *and* **MARC**. *They are outside on the deserted construction site.* **MARC** *crouches over the* **WOMAN,** *who lies in a compromised position.)*

WOMAN. No!

(A loud crack of thunder. The **WOMAN** *lets out a piercing scream.)*

*(***FRANCES,** *her face twisted in rage, gives a primal yell in response.)*

(blackout)

(In the darkness, the sound of **FRANCES** *falling violently.)*

8 SLASHER

Scene One

(Present day. Sound of rain continues.)

(Sound of a car door slamming.)

HILDY. *(offstage)* Wait!

SHEENA. *(offstage)* Run!

(Sound of the two girls squealing as they run through the rain. Sound of keys in the door. Lights up as the front door opens into the living room of an old house. SHEENA and HILDY step into the house, shaking off the storm. They carry a bag of groceries and a box from a chicken joint. FRANCES lies awkwardly on the floor. She wears an old bathrobe and slippers. A motorized scooter sits empty on the other side of the room.)

FRANCES. I've been waiting for you.

SHEENA. *(annoyed)* Jesus Christ.

HILDY. Mom! Are you all right?

SHEENA. What happened.

FRANCES. What do you think happened?

Get my scooter.

*(**HILDY** gets the scooter.)*

SHEENA. Let her get it herself.

FRANCES. Thank you for your concern, Sheena.

SHEENA. The physical therapist showed you how to get up.

FRANCES. According to her I should be training for a damn marathon.

SHEENA. Walking ten minutes three times a day is not –

FRANCES. I FELL.

*(As **HILDY** helps **FRANCES** into the scooter, **SHEENA** reaches into **FRANCES**' pocket, grabs a bottle of pills.)*

SHEENA. How many did you take?

FRANCES. Give me those!

*(**SHEENA** dodges **FRANCES**, counts the pills.)*

I've been lying on the floor for three hours, all you care about is how many pills –

SHEENA. Is today the eleventh?

HILDY. Tenth.

> *(to* **FRANCES** *)*
>
> We got chicken?

FRANCES. It's not enough that I'm disabled, you have to humiliate me, too. Why don't you call Marshall Davis, huh? He would loooove to see me lying on the floor, not able to get up. He'd pay to see that. Get me flat on my back so everybody at city hall can take their turn –

SHEENA. Mother!

FRANCES. STEPPING ON ME.

> You can stop counting. I've been a good little cripple.

SHEENA. Today is the tenth, your prescription was refilled on the first –

FRANCES. So I took an extra –

SHEENA. FOUR extra –

FRANCES. Whatever –

SHEENA. Which is why you were passed out for three hours and forgot to tell me Hildy's practice was cancelled.

FRANCES. It was a choice between taking a couple of extra pills and screaming in agony for half the day! Now give them back.

> *(***SHEENA*** hands ***FRANCES*** the pill bottle.)*

SHEENA. Did you hear from that attorney?

FRANCES. Coward. Ball sucker.

HILDY. You want ice tea?

FRANCES. No thank you, dear.

SHEENA. So he's not taking the case.

FRANCES. Didn't even have the guts to call me himself. Made his secretary do it for him.

SHEENA. Hildy?

HILDY. *(to* **FRANCES** *)* There's mashed potatoes?

> *(***SHEENA*** gathers her things to leave.)*

FRANCES. She's probably not even his secretary. He just employs her so he can claim the blow jobs as a business write off.

SHEENA. Please eat something tonight.

FRANCES. Where are you going?

SHEENA. I picked up a bunch of shifts.

FRANCES. Well, there goes the dean's list.

SHEENA. How else are we going to fix the AC?

FRANCES. You wouldn't have to pick up shifts if they weren't paying you third-world wages –

SHEENA. They're not.

FRANCES. Two dollars and fourteen cents an hour is what women in Mexico make for pulling used limes out of Corona bottles.

SHEENA. I'm late.

FRANCES. You know why they get away with paying you that? Because most tipped workers are WOMEN. If you got the other servers together to protest, stage a walk-out –

SHEENA. We'd be replaced in a day and a half, and then *no one* in this house would have a job.

(to **HILDY***)*

I'm closing tonight, do you have a ride in the morning?

HILDY. Yep.

FRANCES. They underpay you on purpose to force you to giggle and flirt and generally debase yourself so all the dickless little men will leave you a big tip!

SHEENA. I do NOT debase myself!

(IMMEDIATE SHIFT TO:)

Scene Two

*(The bar. **SHEENA** takes off her jacket revealing a tight v-neck T-shirt that reads 'BUSTERS' in big letters across the chest. It's her uniform. She picks up a tray and quickly puts on a big smile for **JODY** and **MARC** who sit at a table in the bar.)*

SHEENA. Hey Jody!

JODY. 'Sup, Sheena.

SHEENA. Be right with you.

*(**SHEENA** exits. **MARC** watches her go uncomfortably, like he's in a dentist's office.)*

JODY. So you were saying?

MARC. I was saying, what I was saying is, that it's an allegory.

JODY. Absolutely –

MARC. Which is the case with most horror movies, the good ones, anyway. They tell us about our deepest fears, not just personally but as a society.

JODY. Definitely.

MARC. Take *Hostel*, right? The whole movie trades on this fear that super rich Europeans *get off* on torturing Americans.

JODY. Well, yeah, but, I mean. They do, right?

*(Beat. **MARC** does not laugh.)*

Just, illustrating your point –

MARC. That's good.

JODY. That we really think rich dudes are total sadists –

MARC. When you let that underlying fear inform every shot, *that's* when you transcend the genre. That's what separates the break-out hit from just another slasher flick – *Texas Chainsaw Massacre* being the original example.

JODY. Oh man, from the word go that film is unbelievable –

MARC. Because of the threat. That's what was so revolutionary.

JODY. Well, that and Tobe Hooper's insane editing – I mean, forty edits per minute –

MARC. Blah blah blah, fine. His editing is great, but it would have meant nothing if he hadn't –. At a time when the media's favorite whipping boy was the so-called 'Me Generation,' he makes a film that says: yes, young people do smoke pot and drink beer and have sex, *but they are innocent.* The threat comes from the adults.

JODY. I see what you mean.

MARC. And not adults like "The Man" or "The Suit," no no no no no. It's the *family.* The movie hits on this deep fear that the family structure itself is ultimately responsible for the most unspeakable violence and terror.

JODY. Absolutely.

MARC. This project I'm working on now, it's really about what happens to a man when he's forced to, to repress and even hate his own, natural, sexual desires.

JODY. Right.

MARC. He should be loving these women – they're beautiful young women – he *wants* to love them, but he's been told that sex is evil. And so he has to kill them.

JODY. Yeah.

(**SHEENA** *re-enters and waits on them.*)

SHEENA. I'm back.

MARC. You are.

SHEENA. What can I get for you?

MARC. Club soda and lime, please.

SHEENA. You got it.

(*to* **JODY**)

And I already know what you want –

(*She starts to exit.*)

JODY. Actually, can I, uh, just get an ice tea?

SHEENA. Um. Sure?

JODY. Thanks.

(**SHEENA** *exits.*)

MARC. You're a regular, huh?

JODY. Well, half the filmmakers in town hang out here, so if you want to know what's going on –

MARC. It's the hub.

JODY. Exactly.

MARC. When I was here there was a place off Magnolia, I hope to God it's been condemned. Can't remember how many times I found McConnoughey or Zellweger passed out on the bathroom floor there –

JODY. Right.

MARC. Oh wait, that was me!

JODY. Right.

MARC. Had a little tendency to, uh, overindulge –

JODY. I've been there, brother.

MARC. But you don't drink anymore?

JODY. Oh. I'll have a beer now and again, just –

MARC. Just not now.

JODY. Well, this is a meeting, right?

MARC. Is it? I mean, you called me, buddy.

JODY. All right, okay, so. So I heard through the grapevine that you need a first assistant.

MARC. Interesting. What else did you hear?

JODY. Nothing, really.

MARC. Uh-huh.

JODY. Well, just that you've got a 21-day shooting permit up in Round Rock that started today, but Jenna Long pulled out of her contract yesterday and took most of your investors with her. But since you're on the hook with the Texas Film Commission and you've already paid up your insurance and deposit on cameras, you're planning to shoot anyway.

MARC. Wow.

JODY. It's a pretty small town.

MARC. Let's assume what you've said is, more or less, true. Why should I give you the job.

JODY. I'm ready, dude. In the past two years I've shot and cut five short films, three of them horror.

MARC. But you've never worked on a feature.

JODY. Well –

MARC. Because, see, here's the thing: if we miss a shot, Jody, if we have to do extra set-ups because someone's not paying attention, I'm literally throwing money away.

JODY. I hear you, brother –

MARC. Not *my* money. But money that I worked very hard to raise. This film gets made in the next twenty days, or it does not get made – and it not getting made is not an option.

JODY. I'm Johnny on the spot –

MARC. You graduate already?

JODY. Um, technically, no, but –

MARC. You're still a student.

JODY. I'm just missing, like, a math class –

MARC. *You can still access the editing room at the University?*

JODY. Oh. Oh! Yeah. Definitely. Access is easy, brother.

MARC. The first assistant is gonna have a lot of responsibility.

JODY. I can handle it.

MARC. And it's gonna be old-school. I'm talking twenty-three hours a day and being grateful for that one hour off. So I need to know: how bad do you want this.

JODY. I'd sell my mom for it.

MARC. Is your mom hot?

JODY. Not really.

MARC. It's a joke.

JODY. Right.

MARC. Sort of.

JODY. Um –

MARC. I'm joking about your mother, specifically – I mean unless you're lying to me and she's one of those really hot moms –

JODY. No.

MARC. Because I have a rule now about not dating anyone under 30, so.

JODY. Oh.

MARC. It's a recent thing.

JODY. I mean, that's cool, man –

MARC. It is. It is cool. You should try it.

JODY. Sure.

MARC. I'm telling you, once you date a woman who is 32 or 33, 35 even? How old are you?

JODY. Twenty-three.

MARC. Talk to me when you've lived in L.A. for fifteen years.

JODY. So does this mean –

(**SHEENA** *brings their drinks.*)

SHEENA. One soda with lime and one ice tea. Can I get y'all anything else right now?

MARC. I'm so sorry I didn't mention this before, but – is it Sheena? I like kind of *a lot* of lime.

SHEENA. Oh –

MARC. I should have said something when I ordered –

SHEENA. Let me get you another one.

MARC. You don't mind?

SHEENA. Not at all! You just want one or two or –

MARC. One will be fine. Thank you.

(**SHEENA** *exits, he watches her go.*)

God, I miss Texas. You have no idea.

JODY. So, the location is in Round Rock?

MARC. It's dynamite. It's suburban and rural all at the same time. I swear to God, find the right location, and you're halfway there.

JODY. I just saw your film, um, *Initiation Rites*? And the locations in that are –

MARC. You what.

JODY. Your movie, from last year?

MARC. How did you, where did you get it.

JODY. I downloaded it.

MARC. Great.

JODY. Did I do something wrong –

MARC. They said they were never going to release it –

JODY. I was just online, and – I mean, you directed that, right, it's yours?

MARC. Did I direct it? Yes, if you can call it "directing" when you're forced to cast five of the six principals with relatives of the investor, and then deal with his demands that entire scenes be re-shot to show his girlfriend at a more flattering angle –

JODY. Yo, I didn't mean to –

(**SHEENA** *brings the lime,* **MARC** *puts up a finger to stop her.*)

MARC. Which I would have done in the first place, if she'd HAD a flattering angle.

(*to* **SHEENA**)

The way you walked across the bar just now to deliver a slice of lime to an agitated but I assure you a very grateful customer – you displayed more intention in that simple action than the lead so-called actress in *Initiation Rites* did for a single moment in the entire movie.

SHEENA. She must've really sucked.

MARC. That, Sheena, is the understatement of the year. The entire film was a waste, except for maybe one shot.

JODY. *The scene in the woods!* With the low angle shot looking up at her. I mean, right?

(*Beat.* **MARC** *sees that* **SHEENA**'*s interested.*)

MARC. Go on.

JODY. It was right after, what was her name –

MARC. *"Gabriella."*

JODY. Right. She's just buried the guy. She takes a step, and the camera is right there. Her bare foot sinks into the mud and you slowly pan up her body. There's blood and dirt caked on her arms and legs, and the trees are towering up behind her. And it's like: she's as powerful and as silent as those trees.

MARC. That's the one.

JODY. It's a great shot.

SHEENA. It sounds cool.

MARC. *(to* **SHEENA**, *this is all for her)* We got on location and it just came to me. That's the thing about directing, you gotta be open all the time, filming in your head constantly, "What if we shoot it this way, what if we put the camera there –"

SHEENA. Right.

JODY. That is so true –

MARC. *(still to* **SHEENA***)* To make a great film, you prepare, you prepare, and then you throw it all out the window and fly.

JODY. Right on, brother.

MARC. Don't say 'brother,' it makes you sound like an asshole.

JODY. Um –

MARC. Scream for me.

SHEENA. Excuse me?

MARC. I'm sorry, I'm being rude. Marc Hunter, I'm a film director.

SHEENA. I figured that out.

MARC. I'm going to be shooting a movie here in town and it just so happens that I need to recast a couple of roles.

SHEENA. Um, I'm not an actress.

MARC. Why don't you let me be the judge of that.

SHEENA. You want me to just scream? Right here in the bar.

MARC. I don't want you to 'just scream.' I want you to scream like...like you're all alone in a house. You're house sitting, friends of your parents. You thought it would be fun. Make your boyfriend a fancy dinner, make love to him in front of the fireplace. But your boyfriend won't be there 'til late and you're upstairs in that king-sized bed, all alone when you hear a noise: drip, drip, drip. It's coming from the attic. You call your boyfriend, he says it's probably just a leak. Get a bucket, he says, and he'll deal with it in the morning. So you find a bucket and a flashlight and ascend the creaking stairs into the deep darkness of the attic. You reach the top of the steps, pull on the light string, and click: the bulb is burned out. You don't want to go, but you have to now. You take a step, flash the light in front of you, and you see a pool of blood, it stretches back to an old wheel chair that's been tipped over, blood gathering beneath it, and there it is, drip, drip, dripping right in front of you and you look up to the rafters and you see it:

SHEENA. *(Screams. It's a knockout.)*

MARC. Yes!

JODY. Wow.

MARC. You were right there, you really saw it –

SHEENA. Holy crap –

MARC. You're brilliant! Pretty but not too pretty, with that believably innocent quality – but at the same time I totally buy that you'd put up a hell of a fight –

JODY. Oh yeah!

MARC. You are the perfect Last Girl.

SHEENA. The last what?

MARC. The Last Girl. The last one to be killed.
     You're not SAG, or AFTRA are you?

SHEENA. What?

JODY. No.

MARC. *(He hands her his card.)* Email me your address, I'll get you a contract tomorrow. Shooting starts Thursday morning.

SHEENA. But, I have class. And I work and –

JODY. So ditch!

SHEENA. I can't just quit my job.

MARC. Well, Sheena, I hate to tear you away from all this, but, um: I'm offering you a role in a feature film.

SHEENA. How much do I get paid?

MARC. The non-union rate is five-hundred a week. Principal shooting starts Thursday, and it goes without saying that you need to be 100 percent available, because as it turns out, time actually is money, and we're already behind schedule.

SHEENA. I want ten grand.

JODY. What?

SHEENA. Ten grand, plus a percentage of gross.

MARC. I'm sorry, the non-union rate is –

SHEENA. I make $500 a week here.

MARC. All right, okay, fair enough.

I'll tell you what: we can do $800 a week.

SHEENA. No.

MARC. We don't normally negotiate this kind of thing –

SHEENA. If I'm the last girl to get killed, that means I'm in most of the movie.

JODY. That's true.

MARC. *(to* **JODY***)* Shut up.

(to **SHEENA***)*

I'll give you fifteen-hundred dollars a week, But that's it –

SHEENA. Ten grand, plus a percentage of gross.

MARC. Only investors get gross!

SHEENA. Then I want twenty grand.

MARC. Okay, did no one ever explain that when you negotiate, the high bidder generally comes down toward the low bidder until you reach a compromise somewhere in the middle?

SHEENA. You just hired a girl in a bar with no experience to play the last girl in your movie? Shooting starts the day after tomorrow, you're already behind schedule and I'm guessing every day you spend looking for a new last girl is gonna cost you a hell of a lot more than twenty grand.

MARC. I'll give you ten grand.

SHEENA. Twenty.

MARC. Ten, plus one percent net –

SHEENA. No –

MARC. Two percent net –

SHEENA. I don't believe in net –

MARC. Fifteen grand, and that's my final offer.

SHEENA. Done.

MARC. Thank God –

JODY. Holy shit –

SHEENA. I'm in the movie?

MARC. Welcome to *Blood Bath*.

SHEENA. Oh my God! I can't believe it! I'm so excited! I have to, I have to go quit my job!

(**SHEENA** *exits.* **MARC** *slams his club soda, gets up.*)

MARC. I have to get out of here, I have to explain to my one remaining investor what the hell just happened.

JODY. But, wait! You never actually said –

MARC. You're in. You'll get gas money, cold tacos on the set and two points net – and don't even think about negotiating.

JODY. You are not gonna regret this, broth – Marc.

MARC. Stop by my hotel in the morning and pick up the script. And start tracking down a meat hook, the biggest claw-foot bathtub you can find, and a wheel chair.

(*Sound of whirring*)

(*IMMEDIATE SHIFT TO:*)

Scene Three

(Frances' house. **FRANCES** *whirs by on her scooter. A knock is heard. She opens the front door to reveal* **CHRISTI**, *who stands holding a clipboard.)*

CHRISTI. Hi, how are you doing today?

FRANCES. That depends, are you Mormon?

CHRISTI. Um, *no –*

FRANCES. I like the Mormons. You can say anything, they just smile.

CHRISTI. I'm Christi Garcia, I'm Assistant Director of the Holy Shepherd Justice League? We're in the area to let people know about an important issue that –

*(***FRANCES*** slams the door in* **CHRISTI**'s *face, cutting her off.* **CHRISTI** *knocks again.* **FRANCES** *opens the door.)*

CHRISTI. Are you aware that there's an abortion clinic being built across the street from the mall? It's going to be six blocks from LBJ high school.

FRANCES. Sounds convenient.

*(***CHRISTI*** hands her a flier.)*

CHRISTI. Holy Shepherd is staging a protest tomorrow, all the information is right here –

FRANCES. What's to protest? Get an abortion, stop for an Orange Julius, still make it to cheerleading practice.

CHRISTI. Cynicism comes from a lack of hope, Mrs…?

FRANCES. *MS.*

CHRISTI. It comes from deep despair. I am living proof of what young people can accomplish when they reject our any-thing-goes culture and embrace the values of self-respect and chastity.

FRANCES. I bet you're a big hit at parties.

CHRISTI. I refuse to stand by and let the cancer of immorality spread unchecked. When you decide you want to take action, when you're ready to help create a better society –

(**FRANCES** *slams the door in her face once more. There is another knock.*)

FRANCES. Look, I already –

(*She opens the door,* **JODY** *is standing there with a script.*)

You're definitely not a Mormon.

(*NOTE: if* **JODY** *looks very clean cut, please change* **FRANCES**' *line to: "Oh good, a Mormon!"*)

JODY. Um, I'm looking for Sheena? I need to drop this off for her. Is she here –

FRANCES. What is this.

(**FRANCES** *grabs the script from him.*)

JODY. The script, for the movie? Are you her mom? Marc asked me to drop it off and –

FRANCES. *Blood Bath.*

JODY. Yeah.

FRANCES. A film by Marc Hunter.

JODY. It's actually not bad –

FRANCES. Marc Hunter –

JODY. A couple of clever twists, and –

FRANCES. Marc with a 'C' –

JODY. He's the –

FRANCES. Smarmy, beady-eyed hustler who went to school here?

JODY. Hey, you know him!

(**FRANCES** *zips into the house, taking the script.*)

(*She pops a handful of pills.*)

JODY. So, okay, I mean, you are Sheena's mom, right? Sheena lives here?

FRANCES. Get out.

(**FRANCES** *starts to charge him.*)

JODY. I'm going, I'm going!

FRANCES. Wait!

(He stops.)

What exactly is Sheena doing with this movie.

JODY. She's in it? She's, like, the main girl.

FRANCES. I see.

JODY. She's gonna be amazing. You should hear her scream.

FRANCES. Oh, I will.

(IMMEDIATE SHIFT TO:)

Scene Four

(Sonic Burger. The car. **SHEENA** *in the driver's seat. She leans out to order into the drive up box.* **HILDY** *sits next to her.)*

DRIVE UP VOICE. *(garbled mess)*

SHEENA. Hi, two chicken strip dinners, an order of chili cheese fries, and two diet cokes please.

DRIVE UP VOICE. *(more garbled mess)*

HILDY. Get something for Mom.

SHEENA. I did. I'm going out, genius.

HILDY. With who?

SHEENA. None of your business.

*(***SHEENA*** *puts on a pair of very hip sunglasses.)*

I do have a life.

HILDY. When did you get those?

SHEENA. Today. I needed a new pair.

HILDY. That why you were so late?

SHEENA. Actually, I was late because I was getting the muffler replaced. The muffler on this car that takes you everywhere – not that you even noticed that you couldn't hear me coming four blocks away.

HILDY. Oh. Yeah, it is a lot quieter!

SHEENA. Look, you need to start taking more responsibility.

HILDY. I already clean the whole house.

SHEENA. For rides, for getting yourself to and from places. I'm not gonna be around forever, so you need to get used to it.

HILDY. What's going on.

SHEENA. What's going on is that I'm 21 years old, I'm supposed to have my own life, not be taking care of you all the time. I'm not your mother.

HILDY. I know that.

SHEENA. Plus I've been cast in a movie.

HILDY. What?!

(**CAR HOP** *arrives with bags of food and drinks.* **SHEENA** *passes them off to* **HILDY,** *gives the* **CAR HOP** *a bill.*)

CAR HOP. Two chicken strip dinners, one chili cheese fry, two diets, nine forty-seven.

HILDY. You're lying!

SHEENA. Here's ten, keep the change.

CAR HOP. Thanks.

(**CAR HOP** *exits.*)

HILDY. You're a marketing major!

SHEENA. So?

HILDY. Seriously?

SHEENA. *Yeah.* The director is in from LA. He came in to Buster's last night with this film guy I kind of know and the next thing, he's offering me a part.

HILDY. It's not porn, is it?

SHEENA. NO!

HILDY. I'm just asking.

SHEENA. It's a horror movie, all right, and I'm the lead, I'm the last girl.

HILDY. The last what?

SHEENA. The last girl, the last to be – I'm basically the main character, so I have to be on the set all the time. You're gonna have to get rides and figure out dinner and stuff.

HILDY. Have you told Mom?

SHEENA. *No,* and you're not going to either.

HILDY. She's gonna freak.

SHEENA. She is a freak.

HILDY. You know how she gets about horror movies –

SHEENA. Which is why no one is telling her.

HILDY. You don't think she's gonna notice you're gone all the time.

SHEENA. Not as long as her prescription doesn't run out.

HILDY. When she finds out, I want to be there to see it.

SHEENA. Do you know how many girls would kill for a chance like this?

HILDY. Oh, sorry, I assumed you were going to *be* killed –

SHEENA. I'm serious!

HILDY. Or forced to saw off your own arms, or get gutted by a maniac or whatever –

SHEENA. *They're paying me fifteen thousand dollars, okay?* Fifteen grand that's gonna fix the AC and pay for your SAT prep course, and get me the hell out of here when I graduate so I don't end up working at Buster's for the rest of my life. So I don't really care right now about Mom's "feminist critique of the horror genre." Because let me tell you something: *It cannot be exploitation when they are paying me this much money.*

HILDY. This is gonna be so rad.

SHEENA. You know what? Tell her. I don't care. She can't stop me. I mean, seriously, she hasn't left the house for almost a year. What's she gonna do?

(IMMEDIATE SHIFT TO:)

Scene Five

*(Frances' house. **HILDY** and **SHEENA** step into the house holding their Cokes and the Sonic bag. **FRANCES** sits on her rascal, ready for battle. She holds the copy of the script.)*

FRANCES. You.

HILDY. Uh-oh.

SHEENA. What is that?

FRANCES. This?

(She rips a single page from the script.)

SHEENA. Don't!

FRANCES. Oh, I thought you didn't know what it was.

SHEENA. Where did you get it.

FRANCES. I was actually hoping that you DIDN'T know –

SHEENA. Give it to me –

FRANCES. Because this, *this* is a chronicle of female degradation, one hundred and five pages in which a virginal young woman named "Sloan" is terrorized –

*(**FRANCES** rips another page.)*

SHEENA. Mother!

FRANCES. *(and another)* sexually objectified –

SHEENA. Stop!

FRANCES. *(and another)* TORTURED AND RAPED AFTER BEING BATHED IN ANOTHER WOMAN'S BLOOD.

HILDY. Gross.

FRANCES. No, Hildy. "Gross" is a booger. "Gross" is vomit, or feces. *This* is a contagion in which the most reprehensible acts are packaged as entertainment – not just entertainment, but as TITILATION, so that men like Marc Hunter will continue to think that it's HOT to see women RAPED AND KILLED! I am going to track him down and cram every single page down his throat, page after page until his dangly little uvula is castrated by a thousand paper cuts and he chokes on his own blood! Or maybe I'll just burn it.

(SHEENA *makes a quick grab for the script, but* FRANCES *zips away on her scooter. A chase.*)

SHEENA. I won't let you!

FRANCES. Where are the matches!

SHEENA. I am doing this movie!

FRANCES. OVER MY DEAD BODY!

SHEENA. I can arrange that!

FRANCES. I will lock you in the closet before I let that happen! I will force-feed you the collected works of Betty Freidan! I will not allow you to be tortured and humiliated –

SHEENA. I WANT TO BE TORTURED, OKAY?

FRANCES. What did you just say.

SHEENA. I want to be tied up, and look scared and scream my head off, and you know why? BECAUSE IT'S A MOVIE.

FRANCES. I am not hearing this.

SHEENA. I AM IN A MOVIE! I'm the STAR! And I didn't just get the part! I NEGOTIATED! I demanded more money and I GOT IT! YOU'RE SUPPOSED TO BE PROUD OF ME!

FRANCES. I'm supposed to be proud you want to be degraded?

SHEENA. IT'S NOT REAL, MOTHER! I'M IN CONTROL!

FRANCES. You're actually retarded, aren't you?

SHEENA. You know what? I'm outta here.

(SHEENA *bounds up the stairs, sound of drawers opening and closing.* FRANCES *comes to the foot of the stairs, talking up at* SHEENA.)

FRANCES. I always knew you weren't smart, but I didn't think you were actually STUPID. Have you learned NOTHING? Watching me bang my head on the glass ceiling, day after day –

(SHEENA *reappears at the top of the stairs.*)

SHEENA. You haven't worked in years.

FRANCES. I HAVE CHRONIC FATIGUE!

SHEENA. You want to stop me from making this movie? Here's your chance: come up here and stop me.

(An expectation.)

FRANCES. Don't mock me.

SHEENA. I dare you. Walk up these stairs and admit that there's nothing wrong with you, and MAYBE I won't do the movie.

HILDY. Sheena, what are you doing?

SHEENA. The choice is yours, Mom.

HILDY. You know she can't go up stairs.

SHEENA. Oh yes she can. She just doesn't want to.

FRANCES. That's not true.

SHEENA. I want you to admit that you're a lazy, bitter drug addict –

HILDY. Sheena, stop it.

SHEENA. Who would rather rail about injustice than GET A JOB –

FRANCES. You're beyond cruel.

SHEENA. What's cruel is pretending you're too tired to even walk across a room, and forcing your daughter to support you so you can spend all your time screaming that you've been discriminated against.

FRANCES. I HAVE been discriminated against –

SHEENA. The city gave Marshall Davis that cleaning contract because you couldn't do the job.

FRANCES. I DID the job.

SHEENA. You took a whole day to clean one floor!

FRANCES. Hello! I'm DISABLED, of course it's going to take me longer.

(**SHEENA.** You are such a victim! God! You talk about how people are so afraid of strong, powerful women "like you." But no one is afraid of you, and you know why? Because you don't DO ANYTHING! Ever since Dad left you've done nothing! Well, I'm actually DOING something now, and you can't stop me.

(**SHEENA** *disappears onto the second floor.*)

FRANCES. Oh, so this is your big statement? Well, I've got a question for you: Who controls the film? Who controls the money, huh? I'll give you a hint: it's not you! You and the rest of your generation, you're all too busy getting boob jobs and counting carbs to notice that WOMEN ARE STILL ROYALLY SCREWED. They pat you on the head, tell you discrimination is over. Who needs equal rights when you've got the WNBA? They trot out Condoleeza Rice once a month like she's the EQUALITY BONG so you're all too stoned to notice that WE STILL ONLY MAKE 76 CENTS ON THE DOLLAR!

(**SHEENA** *barrels down the stairs with a bag of clothes and climbs over* **FRANCES** *like she's a piece of furniture.*)

SHEENA. Get out of my way.

FRANCES. I am not going to let you – OW!

HILDY. Stop it!

FRANCES. You are NOT taking my car.

SHEENA. It's MY car, mom. I bought it after you totaled the last one ramming into Marshall Davis' Expedition!

HILDY. Where are you going?!

FRANCES. If you do this movie, I am disowning you, Sheena. I'll never speak to you again.

HILDY. Mom!

SHEENA. Fine.

HILDY. Sheena!

SHEENA. She's all yours.

HILDY. You can't leave. What am I supposed to do?!

SHEENA. You're the genius. Figure it out.

FRANCES. They've turned my own daughter against me.

SHEENA. No, you did that all on your own.

(*IMMEDIATE SHIFT TO:*)

Scene Six

(Lobby bar. **SHEENA** *approaches* **MARC***, who sits at a table with a club soda and an open bottle of beer.)*

SHEENA. Marc, I'm so sorry to keep you waiting –

MARC. It's okay.

SHEENA. I know it sounds lame, "The dog ate my script," but seriously, if you met my dog –

MARC. It's not a big deal. I've got another copy up in my room.

(catching himself)

Which I will bring down to you. Here.

(He hands her the beer.)

SHEENA. This is for me?

MARC. Well, it's not for me.

SHEENA. You are so nice, and I feel like such a loser! We're supposed to talk about the movie, and acting, and I haven't even read the script –

MARC. No, no, it's better this way. Because here's the thing: I don't want you thinking too much, Sheena. That's the biggest mistake actors make. Over-preparation.

SHEENA. Really?

MARC. Acting is all about being in the moment. They shouldn't even call it "acting." They should call it *reacting.* Because that's what you're doing.

SHEENA. Right.

MARC. It's very instinctual. And that's what you've got. Losing Jenna Long and, honestly, a good chunk of the budget with her, that was, hard to take. But now? I really think you're gonna be better.

SHEENA. Me?

MARC. Absolutely. That's why I wanted to shoot in Texas. I mean, who needs the L.A. attitude when I can find such an unspoiled, untainted, unbelievably attractive, young actress right here.

SHEENA. Um, wow.

MARC. I mean it's also cheaper – it's a lot cheaper. But to this day some of the best work I ever saw and ever did happened right here. Matt McConnoughey didn't know what he was doing any more than the rest of us. We just did it, you know? Filming out of the back of some shitty van, trespassing on construction sites. That's what I'm after with this one.

SHEENA. You know Matthew McConnoughey?

MARC. I know a lot of people.

SHEENA. Oh my God.

MARC. In L.A., that's all anybody cares about: who do you know, who's attached to your project. It has nothing to do with *vision*.

You should move there. As soon as you can.

SHEENA. What?

MARC. I mean, if you're at all interested in having a career as an actress, which I think you could.

SHEENA. Really?

MARC. Absolutely. But if you're gonna do it, don't wait.

SHEENA. Well, I have to finish school.

MARC. No, you don't. I mean, do whatever you want, but L.A. is obsessed with youth. And I hate to say it, but it's especially true for women. The women who wait, or God help them, the ones who go to grad school and THEN move to L.A. when they're 25? They either end up teaching pilates or doing porn.

SHEENA. 25 isn't old.

MARC. How old do you think I am.

SHEENA. I don't know, like, 30?

MARC. I am. I am thirty.

Which is old for a man in L.A., but it's still not as old as a 25-year-old actress.

SHEENA. That's crazy.

MARC. The only unknown 25 year-olds who work get cast as the fat friend. And you, Sheena, are not a fat friend.

SHEENA. There's actually a "fat friend" category?

MARC. Um, *yeah*. It's pretty competitive. There aren't that many fat roles, and, well, nobody wants a fat Pilates instructor, if you know what I'm saying.

SHEENA. *They cast the fat friend in porn?*

MARC. *Niche porn.*

SHEENA. You're making this up.

MARC. I've got pay per view. We can move this conversation up to my room and I'll prove it to you.

(Beat. "Did he say what I think he just said?")

SHEENA. What?

(Beat. "Is she into it? No? No, definitely not.")

MARC. *That's reacting.*

God, you're perfect, so in the moment –

SHEENA. Wait, I was?

MARC. You're gonna be amazing on camera. I want you to remember this, Sheena, this exact moment. How you were open and listening and just ready to react. If you do that on set? I promise you: I will capture it, and you will blow everyone away.

Will you trust me enough to do that?

SHEENA. Yeah, I will.

*(They look at each other. A moment of connection. **MARC** begins to caress her, almost unconsciously. **SHEENA** is unsure how to react.)*

MARC. How's your beer, is it good?

SHEENA. Yeah, I like Shiner.

MARC. Me too.

SHEENA. Oh, I thought you didn't drink.

MARC. I don't. You want another?

SHEENA. That's okay –

MARC. Let me get you another –

SHEENA. Marc, are you trying to get me drunk?

MARC. No! God, no –

SHEENA. I'm just teasing –

MARC. No, I need to attack this head on. I can feel that there's a little attraction happening?

SHEENA. Um –

MARC. But this is a strictly professional relationship, I have absolutely sworn off all, romantic entanglements with women under thirty.

SHEENA. Okay.

MARC. Period. So I've come clean about that. If I hadn't, you know, my sponsor would've crucified me.

SHEENA. I'm so sorry if I was doing something that made you think –

MARC. It's understandable.

SHEENA. I really didn't mean to – I just had this big blow out with my mom, so it's been kind of a crazy day. Almost everything I own is in this bag, I have no idea where I'm even staying tonight, so I'm just a little, whatever –

MARC. You don't know where you're staying?

SHEENA. But starting now, I am one hundred percent professional, Marc. I'm gonna be open, and in the moment, and I will do absolutely everything you tell me to do.

MARC. Well, that's, music to a director's ears.

SHEENA. So should we go up to your room now?

MARC. Um –

SHEENA. I mean, I have to get the script, right?

(IMMEDIATE SHIFT TO:)

Scene Seven

(Frances' house. Night. She sits in her scooter at the table. She's lined up all her pills across the table. A mallet is nearby.)

FRANCES. Marc Hunter. You like to watch. You like to hear women scream, don't you. I should have taken you down when I had the chance. Come on, Frances.

(She counts the pills.)

Onetwothreefourfivesixseveneightnine…Seventeen. Seventeen little lovelies, lovely blues. This was all part of their plan, wasn't it? Keep her doped up, keep her quiet! You have to get rid of them, Frances. Think about him. Sadistic little prick, it all happened because of him and his movie.

Just do it. Do it. DO IT!

*(**FRANCES** swings the mallet, screaming and smashing the pills to bits. **HILDY** runs down the stairs.)*

HILDY. Mom!

FRANCES. AAAAAAARRRRRGGGGHHHHHAAA!

*(**HILDY** watches as **FRANCES** smashes all the pills in a flurry of banging.)*

(an expectation)

HILDY. Why did you just hammer all of your pills?

FRANCES. Because I'm not taking them anymore.

HILDY. What.

FRANCES. I'm done. Finished. Cold turkey.

*(**FRANCES** suddenly puts her face to the table and takes a full snort of the pill powder.)*

FRANCES. Get me the dust buster!

HILDY. What are you –

FRANCES. Now, before I change my mind!

(IMMEDIATE SHIFT TO:)

Scene Eight

(The set. A suburban kitchen. **MARC** *is agitated, pacing.* **JODY** *is on his cell phone. Walkie talkies dangle from both* **MARC** *and* **JODY***'s necks.)*

MARC. Where is he?

JODY. *(to* **MARC***)* He says the directions he got were –

MARC. How far away is he?

JODY. *(into the phone)* How far are you from the set –?

(to **MARC***)*

He doesn't know, he's looking for a place to ask directions but –

MARC. Why didn't he call when he realized he was lost –

JODY. *(overlapping)* He kept thinking it was gonna be –

MARC. Instead of WAITING until he was already late to call –

JODY. *(into the phone)* I know, man, it's cool, it's just –

MARC. IT IS NOT COOL.

JODY. *(into the phone)* Okay, okay, yeah, Perdenales is like –

MARC. Hang up the phone.

JODY. *(into the phone)* I think you're too far South, man, you're –

MARC. *(shouting into his walkie talkie)* I SAID HANG UP THE PHONE.

JODY. *(into the phone.)* I'll call you back.

*(***JODY** *hangs up.* **SHEENA** *has entered, wearing her film costume – a form-fitting tank-top with a bright cropped hoodie, and short shorts.)*

SHEENA. It all fits.

MARC. Great, yes. You look great.

SHEENA. Thanks.

MARC. You look really –. All right, Jody, you're going to stand in for Brian, we're gonna mark through the scene. I'll get all the shots I can of Sheena, while you get back on the phone and see if you can get that idiot here before we get further behind.

JODY. Got it.

MARC. So. You open the door, the first shot is the two of you crossing the threshold, your magical weekend getaway. BRIAN, you find the light switch –

JODY. Over here –

MARC. Yes, and the lights come on and you both look around slowly, slowly. SLOAN, you're nervous, but you're not scared –

SHEENA. Not yet –

MARC. Definitely not. You're excited, you're apprehensive, you want him to like you.

SHEENA. Right.

MARC. BRIAN, you're mostly thinking about how smart you are for getting the keys from your uncle's buddy so you can fuck Sloan's brains out.

JODY. Got it.

MARC. But in a sweet way. Hit this mark, we'll do a nice 360 around the two of you, thinking all of these things, so we see how harmless and normal the place looks.

JODY. Right.

MARC. Then BRIAN, hit your mark here for the line, "See? What did I tell you?"

JODY. Right.

MARC. SLOAN you stay right here, still a little apprehensive.

(**MARC** *demonstrates for* **SHEENA.**)

"Are you sure he said it was okay? You hardly know this guy."

(*to* **JODY**)

Brian:

JODY. *(in a leading man voice)* "He gave me the key, didn't he?"

MARC. Yes. Grab hands.

JODY. "Don't worry, he's out of town until Monday. We've got the place all to ourselves."

SHEENA. *(imitating* **MARC***'s vocal quality and body language)* "Until everybody else gets here."

MARC. Good.

JODY. "It'll be fun."

SHEENA. "I know. I just wanted this weekend to be…special."

JODY. "It will be. I promise."

MARC. And the shot goes back to Sloan as Brian moves to the next room.

JODY. "Come on, check it out."

MARC. *(to* **SHEENA***)* The camera's still on you, scanning your face, you decide to follow your man, and walk out of the shot.

(**JODY***'s phone rings.*)

JODY. It's him.

MARC. Go.

(**JODY** *steps away to answer the phone.*)

MARC. Once he's gone –

SHEENA. Look, before Jody comes back – I just wanted to say thanks, again, for letting me crash in your room last night.

MARC. Don't mention it.

SHEENA. You totally saved me, and I really didn't intend to impose, or make you uncomfortable –

MARC. I was, totally comfortable. I mean it's not like we were sleeping together!

SHEENA. No! I know!

MARC. I mean, they give you two beds, someone may as well use the, the other one.

SHEENA. I just I wanted to say thanks. I got a hold of my friend Heather, I'm gonna stay with her now –

MARC. Great. That's great –

SHEENA. So it won't happen again.

MARC. Well, you know, any time you want to you can always, always –. Let's skip ahead. Madison calls, she's having car trouble, they're gonna be late. You and Brian have been playing hide and seek. It's sexy, it's playful – at some point you lose the jacket?

SHEENA. *(She takes off the jacket.)* Right.

MARC. So you're exploring the house. Something seems strange, and now you can't find Brian. Is this part of the game? Maybe. You step in here to look, hit this mark.

SHEENA. *(in her movie voice)* "Brian? Come on, where are you?"

MARC. The room is empty. You notice the family photos: a stern minister with a very young Victor and the beautiful Elise, *who you realize looks almost exactly like you.* You see the framed newspaper clipping about Elise's death. A cold wind blows through the room. You shudder, and turn and see: the door to the porch is mysteriously open. You hit this mark here. Now you're getting worried.

SHEENA. "Brian?"

MARC. You hear a noise. You go to the porch, but it's not coming from there. What is it? Your senses are on high alert, your nipples should be like rocks.

SHEENA. What?

MARC. Skip it. You shut the door, shivering. You listen, trying to figure out where the noise is coming from. You hear it, coming from in here. But that can't be, that's impossible. Hit this mark –

SHEENA. "Come on, this isn't funny."

MARC. Open the door and –

(**SHEENA** *opens the door to reveal* **BRIDGET**, *a brunette. She's virtually naked and her neck and wrists have been slit.)*

(*NOTE: Some productions have concealed* **BRIDGET** *in a giant freezer, with* **BRIDGET** *spilling out onto the floor*

like a corpse. Others have used a closet, with **BRIDGET**
*hanging upside down as if she's been trussed up there to
let her blood drain. I'm sure there are other possibilities
as well.)*

SHEENA. *(screams)*

MARC. *YES!*

SHEENA. Oh my God.

BRIDGET. Hey. I'm Bridget.

MARC. Oh, I'm sorry, did you guys not meet yet?

SHEENA. No.

MARC. Bridget's dead girl number one.

BRIDGET. The unsuspecting realtor who gets it in the first
ten minutes.

SHEENA. Right. Nice to meet you.

MARC. *(to* **SHEENA***)* That reminds me: You're not claustro-
phobic, are you?

SHEENA. Um –

(*IMMEDIATE SHIFT TO:*)

Scene Nine

*(Frances' house. **FRANCES** is on the phone. She digs through an old toolbox as she waits to leave a message. Some tools she considers and then discards back into the toolbox. When she finds a tool she likes, she sets it out on the table, like a surgeon assembling her instruments.)*

*(Just as **FRANCES** beings to leave the message, **HILDY** enters with a sad-looking pair of soccer shoes. When she hears **FRANCES** speak, she stops short, unseen by **FRANCES**. As **HILDY** listens, she slowly backs away, becoming more and more anxious.)*

FRANCES. Mr. Hunter, this is Belinda Chapman from Channel 5 News. I'm a, real *fan* of your work, all the way back to your earliest days here in Austin.

(She finds a hatchet, hefts it in her hand, sets it on the table.)

Oh yes. And I would LOVE to interview you about your new project. *Blood Bath?* I have to say, it sounds like a real crowd pleaser.

(She snaps a large needle nose pliers in then air, adds them to her selected tools.)

So, I thought we'd meet at the set. I think that'd be best. I really want to get an up-close look at your –

(She revs a cordless drill.)

artistic process. I am really looking forward to this. You name the time, Mr. Hunter. And I will be there.

*(**HILDY** pulls out her phone, dials frantically.)*

(IMMEDIATE SHIFT TO:)

Scene Ten

(Break room. The set. **SHEENA** *and* **MARCY**. **SHEENA**
*is still in her costume, and now has mud streaks up her
legs.* **MARCY** *is a redhead who appears to have had half
her face burned off. The other half of her face is perfect.
They drink Diet Cokes and eat chips. An occasional
SCREAM is heard – filming continues nearby.)*

MARCY. God, I can't wait to get home and wash this stuff
off.

SHEENA. I bet.

(A scream is heard. They continue their conversation.)

MARCY. Amanda's good, though. I mean this stuff she did
on my face, with the burns –

SHEENA. It's, amazing.

MARCY. It totally looks like someone held me down on a
hot griddle. Which is good, because, you know, I was
held down on a hot griddle!

SHEENA. Right.

*(**SHEENA***'s phone rings, she silences it.)*

MARCY. So when do you get killed?

SHEENA. Um, later. At the end, actually.

MARCY. You're the last girl?

SHEENA. Yeah.

MARCY. Wow, that's gotta be cool. How do they do it?

SHEENA. I get impaled, I think.

MARCY. Awesome. Save the best for last, right?

SHEENA. Marc said it might change, but I think I get to
take Victor down with me.

(Her phone rings again, she silences it.)

He's been keeping me chained up while he kills everyone else, because I look like his dead sister?

MARCY. Uh-huh.

*(More screaming, **SHEENA** talks over it.)*

SHEENA. After he washes me in all the blood he's collected, he wants to put me in one of Elise's old dresses. That's when I make a break for it. He comes after me and we end up crashing through the railing, and I fall and get impaled on the same spike as Brian. Victor freaks, 'cause he wasn't gonna kill me, he was gonna keep me? So it's like I'm Elise dying all over again. And while he's trying to keep me from bleeding out, I grab his knife and gut him!

MARCY. Cool!

SHEENA. *(Her phone rings again.)* Ugh.

MARCY. Someone really wants to talk to you.

SHEENA. It's my sister. She's been calling all day because my mom is, my mom is crazy.

MARCY. I totally know what you mean.

SHEENA. No, I mean, she's literally *crazy.* And I feel bad my sister has to deal with her, but, I just, I need a break from it all.

(Sound of a chainsaw. A **WOMAN** *screams, "No, no, please!")*

I need to have some normalcy for once, you know?

MARCY. Totally.

SHEENA. My sister's probably freaking out about some stupid thing my mom is saying she's gonna do. But she never actually DOES anything. She's all talk. And if I answer, I'm just gonna get sucked back in.

MARCY. Then I say don't do it.

SHEENA. I deserve to have some fun, right?

MARCY. Hell yeah! Oh, crap.

SHEENA. What?

MARCY. *(***MARCY** *pulls something out of her mouth.)* Part of my burn flaked off.

SHEENA. Let me see.

MARCY. Amanda's gonna kill me.

SHEENA. Oh, I'm sure she can fix it.

MARCY. I better go. I'll see you.

    *(**SHEENA**'s phone rings again, she silences it.)*

    (IMMEDIATE SHIFT TO:)

Scene Eleven

*(**HILDY**, on the phone in a tight light – she is hiding somewhere in the house.)*

HILDY. Sheena? Look, I know you're busy being mutilated and all, but seriously, Mom has flipped her can. She stopped taking her pills, Sheena. Mom is SOBER. She got dad's old tools and set up target practice with the staple gun, and now she's making me help her build explosives! She wants to blow up the guy who's directing the movie. She keeps talking about how she's not gonna be a joke on the ten o'clock news this time? I seriously think she's gonna do something so please pick up your freakin' phone!

FRANCES. *(offstage)* Hildy!

HILDY. I'm freaking out, I don't know what to do and I need new soccer shoes by Friday! Call me.

FRANCES. *(offstage)* Hildy come here!

*(**HILDY** sneaks out of her spot and enters the living room where **FRANCES** sits, in her scooter.)*

HILDY. I'm right here, Mom.

FRANCES. Where?

*(There is a board with wires sticking out of it on the table now, along with an assortment of tools and plastic bottles – a ridiculous attempt to make a bomb. **FRANCES** is a wreck, she's twitching and shaking. The rumpled remains of the script, and the Holy Shepherd flier are strewn about. **HILDY** stands out of **FRANCES**' line of vision, packing her backpack, putting on her bike helmet.)*

HILDY. I was looking for more plastic.

FRANCES. Get it and let's finish.

HILDY. Um, I have to go to school, Mom.

FRANCES. Screw school!

HILDY. You're shaking.

FRANCES. Just ignore it.

HILDY. And sweating a lot –

FRANCES. It'll stop in a minute.

HILDY. I really think I should call Dr. Mosier –

FRANCES. NO! That pill-pushing prick. He's practically been force-feeding me narcotics for the last fifteen years! Trying to keep me from DOING SOMETHING. Well, NOT ANYMORE.

HILDY. Okay, Mom: I know this is not really about fixing the toaster.

FRANCES. Keep working.

HILDY. You could go to jail for building a bomb.

FRANCES. Bomb? Who said anything about a bomb.

HILDY. The instructions you printed off the internet say it. Look, I know you're upset about Sheena and the movie, but I mean you've already got a deferred sentence for trying to run over Marshall Davis after he got the cleaning contract –

FRANCES. I THOUGHT I WAS PRESSING THE BRAKE.

HILDY. If you try to blow up this director they are gonna put you away.

FRANCES. Do you know how many crimes go unsolved each year? How many criminals are never brought to justice? Murderers and rapists –

HILDY. Mom –

FRANCES. HUNDREDS. THOUSANDS. Half the time the police don't even LOOK.

HILDY. I think they're gonna look for a bomber.

FRANCES. If they'd been looking, they would have caught him before it happened again! Then that self-righteous dyke getting on the news saying I should have done something. Well NOW, I am going to DO SOMETHING. And this time, NO ONE is going to be LAUGHING!

(**HILDY** *has quietly taken the key to* **FRANCES**' *scooter.*)

What are you doing. Hey! HEY!

(**HILDY** *stands out of reach, holding the key.*)

HILDY. I'm taking your key, I swear this is for your own good.

(**FRANCES** *reflexively presses the button on her chair; nothing happens. A moment of horror.*)

FRANCES. *Give it back.*

HILDY. I'm going to school.

FRANCES. Give me my key!

HILDY. Promise you'll just stay here until I get back, okay?

FRANCES. Hildegard McKinney –

HILDY. *I don't think you're faking.*

Okay? I know Sheena does, and a lot of other people. My friends, and most of my teachers. Coach Conner –

FRANCES. That health Nazi always hated me –

HILDY. But if you were only pretending to be disabled, that would mean that all this time – my whole life basically – you've never been there. That you've never come to any of my soccer games or the awards assembly or anything, not because you couldn't but because you didn't want to.

FRANCES. Hildy, you know that's not true –

HILDY. *(overlapping)* And I know that's not true! You want to be a good Mom, it's just. You're in a lot of pain. Right?

(an expectation)

FRANCES. I hurt *so much.*

HILDY. I know.

FRANCES. I never wanted to be like this. They did this to me. You see that, don't you? Things were supposed to get better –

HILDY. They will –

FRANCES. No, no, they won't, not unless we do something –

HILDY. I'm taking your key, okay?

FRANCES. We have to stop them, Hildy –

HILDY. Because then you'll be safe here. Because you can't go anywhere without your chair, right?

FRANCES. You're so smart, I know we can do it –

HILDY. So I'm putting a bottle of water, and, and a Hot
    Pocket on the table for you –

FRANCES. We can finish it!

HILDY. I'll just be at school –

FRANCES. Don't leave me!

(**HILDY** *turns on the radio.*)

HILDY. You can listen to the news, and when I get home –

FRANCES. We have to take a stand –

HILDY. I'll be back, I swear.

FRANCES. Hildy, don't go, don't –

(**HILDY** *exits.*)

FRANCES. HILDY!

Stupid internet instructions!

Think. Think, Frances.

RADIO. …In breaking news, a bomb went off this morn-
    ing at the site of the proposed Emma Goldman clinic
    on Payne Avenue. Anti-abortion protesters organized
    by Holy Shepherd Church gathered at the site last
    night in an effort to prevent the clinic from opening.
    In a statement released earlier today, church leaders
    denied any involvement in the bombing. Fortunately,
    no one was injured. In other news…

(**FRANCES** *springs into action. She grabs the phone cord,
pulls it to her. She finds the Holy Shepherd flier, dials the
number, waits for someone to pick up.*)

FRANCES. Yes, may I speak to –

(*She refers to the sheet of paper.*)

Christi Garcia? Thank you, I'll hold.

(*IMMEDIATE SHIFT TO:*)

Scene Twelve

(The set. **BETH**, *a blonde in soccer mom clothes strides onto the set where* **MARC** *is getting* **JODY** *in to costume and instructing him.)*

MARC. *(to* **JODY***)* Keep your face front, so we get a good shot of the mask, that's the most important thing.

JODY. Right –

BETH. Where the hell is Tyler?

MARC. He's been replaced, all right?

BETH. Jesus Christ.

MARC. Why is this so baggy?

JODY. Dude, Tyler was a lot bigger than me, but maybe I can –

MARC. Lose it. Just go with the mask.

JODY. Yeah.

*(***SHEENA** *enters, watches.)*

MARC. When you start pushing her through the saw, make sure you really sell it, I want to see how much effort it takes to cut through her skull.

JODY. Got it.

SHEENA. Where's Tyler? Why is Jody dressed like Victor now?

BETH. Didn't you hear? It's amateur night.

MARC. *(to* **BETH***)* It's gonna be fine!

BETH. Sorry, Mr. Scorsese.

(to **SHEENA***)*

I'm so moving to L.A., just as soon as I finish grad school.

MARC. Let's get set up for the take. Get your mask on, SLOAN'S MOM, get into position.

*(***JODY** *puts on a creepy mask, while* **BETH/SLOAN'S MOM** *slips her arms through two ropes attached to a table so that she appears to be tied down.)*

JODY. Do you want me to say the lines?

MARC. Yeah – just keep the scene going. We'll dub it later if we have to.

(MARC's phone rings. He hands it to SHEENA.)

Damnit – this is that reporter again. Find out when she's coming for the interview.

SHEENA. Sure –

(SHEENA stuffs the phone in her armpit and runs for an exit.)

MARC. *(into his walkie)* Standing by.

JODY. *(grabbing his walkie from his back pocket)* Standing by.

(He stuffs it back in his pocket.)

MARC. And action!

BETH/SLOAN'S MOM. I know you have my daughter, and you won't get away with it!

(Sound of the circular saw starts as SHEENA steps off the set into a tight spotlight. Lights go out on the set, but we continue to hear the sound of the saw and screaming as filming continues.)

SHEENA. *(into the phone)* Hello? Hello?

(She's missed the call.)

Crap.

(She looks at the number to redial and sees:)

Oh my God….Mom?!?

(IMMEDIATE SHIFT TO:)

Scene Thirteen

*(Frances' house. Sound of knocking. **FRANCES** crawls or rolls across the floor to the door. She opens it, revealing **CHRISTI**, who carries her clipboard and some brochures.)*

FRANCES. What took you so long?

CHRISTI. I was a little tied up.

FRANCES. Well don't just stand there, come in.

*(**CHRISTI** awkwardly steps over **FRANCES**.)*

CHRISTI. I must say, I was surprised you called me, Ms. McKinney.

FRANCES. You're not the only one.

CHRISTI. The Lord works in mysterious ways.

*(She watches **FRANCES** struggle for a moment.)*

Can I help you up, or –

FRANCES. I'm FINE.

CHRISTI. All right then. I brought some information about Holy Shepherd, and of course, the information about the Justice League that you requested. I also wanted to let you know about our pick up service, Riders to Joy? We have two transport vans that are fully handicap accessible and –

FRANCES. Are you driving one now?

CHRISTI. Um, no ma'am. I'm driving my personal vehicle?

FRANCES. That's all right, that'll work.

CHRISTI. Excuse me?

FRANCES. Look, let's cut to the chase. I called you because I want to stop this.

*(She hands **CHRISTI** the script.)*

It's despicable.

CHRISTI. *Blood Bath.* These movies are just awful.

FRANCES. We have to stop them. Every other minute there's a Law and Order with a prostitute dead in an alley, a CSI with a stripper face down in a vat of Jell-O –

CHRISTI. You're shaking a little, are you okay?

FRANCES. Sometimes I think if I see one more "artistic" shot of a beautiful young woman who's been beaten or tortured or raped, I will go completely crazy.

CHRISTI. Don't you worry. The Justice League has a plan.

FRANCES. What are we gonna do.

CHRISTI. We have a letter you can send to your local TV stations and movie theatres –

FRANCES. No no no –

CHRISTI. When advertisers hear from consumers –

FRANCES. Nobody pays attention to that stuff –

CHRISTI. When they see an effect on the bottom line –

FRANCES. I'm talking about fire bombs!

CHRISTI. What.

FRANCES. Why the hell do you think I called you? I heard about the bombing this morning –

CHRISTI. Ms. McKinney –

FRANCES. You people know how to get shit done, and you get away with it, too!

CHRISTI. Pastor Dan issued a statement, Holy Shepherd had NOTHING to do with that –

FRANCES. I want to kill him. The director, the producer, everyone who's involved –

CHRISTI. We do not advocate the use of violence as a means to –

FRANCES. You don't have to pretend with me –

CHRISTI. The Justice League is not –

FRANCES. By any means necessary!

We may not agree on everything, but you and I both know that letters won't change anything. We have to *do something* to get their attention. My daughter has been brainwashed by this, this trash, and I'm gonna lose her. We have to stop them. We have to save them.

CHRISTI. What did you have in mind?

FRANCES. I know where they're filming. I got the director's number off the script, and said I was from Channel Five. Then he sang like a canary. The house is half a mile from your church. All I need is a ride.

(an expectation)

CHRISTI. Is that mess of wires supposed to be a bomb?

FRANCES. You tell me.

*(Spilt Scene: The Set. **SHEENA** runs into an isolated place, she has twigs sticking out of her hair, like she's been running through the woods.)*

JODY. *(offstage)* Sheena?

SHEENA. *(calling off to **JODY**)* Just a second!

(to herself)

I have to check my messages.

*(**CHRISTI** and **SHEENA** dial their phones.)*

FRANCES. Who are you calling?

CHRISTI. My friend Piper. Her dad's an explosives expert at the ATF?

(She waits for Piper to pick up.)

Since Pastor Dan hired me, I've implemented a three-hundred and sixty degree strategy that includes outreach, publicity, utilization of the courts, and covert ops.

SHEENA. *(as she listens to **HILDY**'s message)* Oh my God.

FRANCES. *Covert ops.*

CHRISTI. *(to the phone)* Hey Piper, it's Christi, call me back, 'k?

SHEENA. *Oh my God!*

*(**CHRISTI** hangs up.)*

FRANCES. You're like a perky little general.

CHRISTI. That's what it takes to battle evil. And we're gonna strike at the source.

SHEENA. *Oh my freakin' God!*

(IMMEDIATE SHIFT TO:)

Scene Fourteen

(The set. **SHEENA** *runs to* **JODY**.*)*

SHEENA. Jody! Look, I need your help –

JODY. As soon as Marc is done with Madison, you need to be in position for the chase –

SHEENA. Listen to me. Marc thinks someone from Channel Five is coming.

JODY. Yeah, I talked to her earlier.

SHEENA. Did you tell her where we are, she *knows* where the location is?

JODY. Yeah.

SHEENA. Crap. I have to go.

JODY. What?!

SHEENA. I'm sorry but this is –

JODY. They're gonna be done any minute!

SHEENA. I think my mom wants to kill Marc!

JODY. What?

MARC. *(offstage) (coming through the walkie around* **JODY**'s *neck) Quiet on the set!*

SHEENA. I should have answered my phone –

JODY. What are you talking about?

SHEENA. He's the guy! He's – seriously, she thinks he ruined her life!

JODY. Marc?

SHEENA. Yes! He was making this movie – he must have been in college. He snuck onto my dad's construction site because he was filming there at night –

JODY. Right.

SHEENA. There'd been a whole series of rapes that summer. It was all over the news. My mom was obsessed, she was part of this women's action group? So one night my dad doesn't come home – probably because he's off with his secretary. My mom goes to the construction site to try to find him. When she gets there she hears this woman screaming. She sees all these people standing around, so she calls the cops –

JODY. Because she thinks –

SHEENA. Yes! And then she calls the TV station and says: the Austin serial rapist is here, right now! The cops are about to nab him, here's the address!

JODY. Nooo –

SHEENA. The TV crews get there first, and all they find is Marc and a bunch of kids filming this scene. It becomes a big joke on the 10 o'clock news. And that night another woman is raped! The cops say if my mom hadn't called in a false report they would've caught the guy.

JODY. Whoa.

SHEENA. And this bitch from the women's group gets on the news and says if my mom really thought a woman was being raped, she should have done more to stop them. My mom completely loses it, my dad runs off with his secretary and now I'm making a movie with the SAME GUY.

JODY. Holy coincidence, Batman.

SHEENA. She's making my little sister try to build a – she's gonna try to kill him.

JODY. Okay, isn't your mom, like, in a wheelchair?

SHEENA. Look, I will be back as soon as I can –

(SHEENA *turns and runs smack into* CHRISTI.)

(*screams*)

CHRISTI. There's gonna be a lot less of that going on now.

(*She gives a card to* JODY.)

Christi Garcia, Assistant Director of the Holy Shepherd Justice League.

(MARC *comes running in behind her.*)

MARC. I told you, this is a closed set.

CHRISTI. I just wanted to let the rest of your crew know that filming is about to shut down.

JODY. What?

CHRISTI. Holy Shepherd has filed an injunction barring you from using this property on behalf of the owner.

(She produces a document.)

JODY. We have all the permits!

CHRISTI. Mr. Parrish didn't understand the nature of the movie you all would be making here.

MARC. He understood the money I paid him to use this dump!

CHRISTI. We'll have you shut down by Monday, so it really would be best for you to just leave now.

(to **SHEENA***)*

You know, you don't have to take your clothes off to make people like you.

SHEENA. Excuse me?!

CHRISTI. But first you have to like yourself.

MARC. Look, unless you flash a badge in the next three seconds –

CHRISTI. Mr. Parrish is a member of Holy Shepherd –

MARC. *(to* **JODY***)* Call the cops, dial 911, RIGHT NOW.

*(***JODY** *dials.)*

CHRISTI. There's no need, I'm leaving. But I'll be back. Judge Monson is scheduled to hear the case first thing Monday morning. He's a very fair man. I should know. He's my Uncle.

(hands **SHEENA** *a card)*

When you're ready to treat yourself with respect, close your legs and call me.

*(***CHRISTI** *exits as* **SHEENA** *shouts after her.)*

SHEENA. Hey!

MARC. Sheena, find Amanda, tell her we're skipping ahead –

SHEENA. Marc –

MARC. Tell her she has to do all of Madison's make-up and wounds for the meat hook scene *now.*

JODY. The meat hook scene?

SHEENA. Marc, I have to go home.

MARC. What?

JODY. That's almost at the end of the movie!

SHEENA. I know it's bad timing, but –

MARC. No one's going anywhere.

SHEENA. But it's an emergency!

MARC. You leave, I will come after you for delay of production and take every cent you've got.

(to **JODY**)

Jody, anything that can be shot someplace else, take it off the schedule. Make sure we've got all the exteriors –

JODY. Look, I'm all about working fast, but –

MARC. Good –

JODY. We've only been shooting for two days!

MARC. We have to work faster –

JODY. We barely have enough footage to cover 20 minutes of film –

MARC. So get moving!

JODY. Just call your investor and ask him to –

MARC. *There is no investor!* All right? I am financing this entire movie with a three-hundred-thousand dollar second mortgage on my six-hundred square foot condo, most of which is already spent! And I will be damned if I am going to be homeless at thirty-seven years old!

SHEENA. You're thirty-seven?

MARC. NO! Now we are going to shoot enough film in the next forty eight hours to edit together SOMETHING that I can sell to a video distributor, even if it kills me. So until the cops show up to shut us down, *nobody leaves the set.* Now move!

(IMMEDIATE SHIFT TO:)

Scene Fifteen

(Split scene. **SHEENA** *steps downstage into a spotlight, pulls out her phone and dials as:)*

*(***HILDY** *enters the house, wearing her backpack and bike helmet.)*

HILDY. Mom? Mom?

(She sees the empty scooter.)

Crap!

(Her phone rings. She answers it.)

HILDY. Oh my God, Sheena –

SHEENA. I just got your messages and –

HILDY. I swear to God, I didn't think she could leave –

SHEENA. What?

HILDY. You said it yourself, she hasn't left in a year, and I had to go to school –

SHEENA. What's happening?

HILDY. She's gone! She's not here –

SHEENA. What?!

HILDY. I really didn't think she could do it, I even took her key! Her scooter's still here, but she's gone –

SHEENA. She was building a bomb and you left her alone?!

HILDY. I had a chemistry quiz!

SHEENA. Okay, all right. She couldn't have gotten very far, right? she doesn't have money for a cab, I have the car. Even if she's planning to blow up Marc, she'd have no way of getting here, right?

*(***HILDY** *finds the flier from Holy Shepherd.)*

MARC. *(offstage)* Sheena! Get in here!

HILDY. This is weird.

SHEENA. What?

HILDY. It's just, this flier. It's from some church group, she circled the phone number over and over.

SHEENA. Oh my God, what's the name of the church?

HILDY. Holy Shepherd? It's for something called the Justice League.

SHEENA. Crap.

MARC. *(offstage)* SHEENA!

(IMMEDIATE SHIFT TO:)

Scene Sixteen

(Break room. The set. **MADISON**, *a perky blonde, sits alone in a prop wheelchair, listening to her headphones. She sings to herself, an up-beat pop song like "Love Shack" by B-52s.* She has what appears to be a gigantic meat hook going through her back and out her chest.)*

MADISON. *(singing)* …the love shack is…we can get to-ge-ther-er…

*(***FRANCES*** appears behind* **MADISON**, *doing a commando-style crawl, advancing on* **MADISON**.*)*

MADISON. *(in a low voice)* Love Shack Baby.

*(***FRANCES*** has outfitted herself with an old tool belt containing various tools that could be used as weapons.* **FRANCES** *crawls up behind* **MADISON**, *waiting for her opportunity.)*

MADISON. *(still singing)* Bang bang bang on the door baby… I can't hear you.
BANG BAN-GGGAAAAAHHH!!!

(As **MADISON***'s mouth opens wide,* **FRANCES** *stuffs a bandana in it, stifling her scream.)*

(IMMEDIATE SHIFT TO:)

---

* Please see Music Use Note on Page 3.

Scene Seventeen

(The set. A tight light follows **SHEENA**, *as though she is being tracked by a camera. They are filming. She runs a few steps, trips and falls.)*

SHEENA/SLOAN. *(in her movie voice)* "No!"

(She turns back towards her pursuer, pushing herself away from him. **JODY**, *dressed as* **VICTOR**, *advances menacingly towards her, wearing his signature mask.* **SHEENA** *remains on the floor, backing herself into a corner.)*

SHEENA/SLOAN. "No, no please –"

JODY/VICTOR. "Oh yes."

*(**VICTOR** reaches **SHEENA**, grabs her –)*

SHEENA/SLOAN. *(screams)*

(She struggles to get away, but **VICTOR** *handcuffs* **SHEENA** *to an old radiator. She whimpers and cries.)*

SHEENA/SLOAN. "No no no no"

JODY/VICTOR. "You shouldn't have worn this. You knew daddy wouldn't like it."

(In a swift movement, **VICTOR** *rips* **SHEENA***'s shirt down the center, leaving her stomach and chest exposed except for her bra.)*

JODY/VICTOR. "Now it's time for your bath."

(The light follows **VICTOR** *as he turns to a bathtub of blood. Above it is an empty harness where* **MADISON** *is supposed to be.)*

MARC. CUT. Where the hell is Madison? She's supposed to be in the shot!

JODY. I told her to get in position ten minutes ago –

MARC. *(calling)* MADISON!

SHEENA. You want us to reset –

MARC. *NO.* Stay where you are, we can take it from the reveal –

(*calling*)

MADISON IF YOU DON'T GET ON THIS MEAT HOOK IN THE NEXT 60 SECONDS –

(*All the lights go out.*)

JODY. What the –

SHEENA. Oh my God.

MARC. Great. This is just great.

SHEENA. Marc, there's something I should tell you.

MARC. Did you see the fuse box in the laundry room?

JODY. I'm already on my way –

SHEENA. No! Wait, please –

MARC. GO.

(JODY *exits.*)

SHEENA. Marc, you have to unlock me.

MARC. Just STAY WHERE YOU ARE.

SHEENA. Seriously, I have a really bad feeling about this.

(MARC *laughs.*)

I didn't tell you before because I didn't want you to think I was crazy, but –

MARC. (*He laughs more.*) You have a *bad feeling* about this?

SHEENA. Listen to me –

MARC. I lost my star, all my investors, quite possibly the only piece of property I'l ever owned, and you have a BAD FEELING?

SHEENA. I THINK MY MOTHER IS HERE!

(*The lights flick on.* FRANCES *is there, in the wheelchair. She wears a hockey mask, a la Jason from Friday the 13th, her hand on her holstered cordless drill.*)

SHEENA. (*screams*)

FRANCES. Hello, Marc.

MARC. Who are you?

SHEENA. Mom, please!

MARC. Wait, this is your mother?

(**FRANCES** *takes the mask off.*)

FRANCES. We'll see who's laughing in five minutes.

MARC. I'm sorry, you can stay for a couple of takes, but you've got to keep quiet and stay out of the way.

FRANCES. You'd like that wouldn't you?

SHEENA. Nobody wants you here, so just leave!

FRANCES. Keep us all tied up and whimpering, like Sheena.

(*to* **SHEENA**)

You're really in control now.

SHEENA. I *am* in control!

MARC. Do I know you?

FRANCES. If it weren't for me, you wouldn't even have your pathetic little career –

SHEENA. We'll call the police.

FRANCES. You'd still be working construction, but thanks to all the free publicity –

MARC. Wait a minute –

FRANCES. I should have done this fifteen years ago.

MARC. (*it dawns on him*) You!

FRANCES. That's right.

The middle of the night, a woman is dragged to a construction site, beaten and raped –

MARC. It was a movie!

FRANCES. I forgot, it's all okay because it isn't REAL. It's in SERVICE of the STORY. Isn't that what you said to Channel Five? "It's not about depicting violence against women, it's about telling the story!"

MARC. Well, yeah!

FRANCES. DID YOU EVER STOP TO THINK THAT MAYBE WE NEED SOME DIFFERENT STORIES?!?!

(**MARC** *attempts to leave the room,* **FRANCES** *maneuvers to stop him, revving the drill.*)

FRANCES. Oh no you don't. I want justice, and this time I'm gonna get it.

SHEENA. You can't stop us!

FRANCES. I've already taken down everyone else in the place.

MARC. What.

FRANCES. Your bloody little bimbos, that punk who came to the house –

SHEENA. What did you do?

FRANCES. The make up girl? She was spunky.

MARC. *(calling)* Jody!

SHEENA. Mother, they will put you away for this!

MARC. I'm calling the cops.

(MARC starts to dial, FRANCES trips him, his phone goes flying. She points the drill at him like a gun.)

FRANCES. DON'T MOVE!

(MARC holds his hands up in spite of himself. JODY creeps into the room unseen by FRANCES. He has several bleeding cuts on his arms, and duct tape wrapped around his head. SHEENA sees JODY, they silently make a quick plan.)

I can't let you do this, Sheena. You were supposed to finish what we started. But you just take whatever they force on you and then pretend it's what you wanted in the first place!

SHEENA. It IS what I want!

FRANCES. You're dragging us all back down!

SHEENA. I am pulling myself up! You know why there are so many horror movies? BECAUSE PEOPLE LIKE THEM! That's it!

(MARC see JODY.)

It's not some huge conspiracy to degrade women, or keep women down. Because the last time I checked, women have all the same rights as men! If a woman doesn't get a job, it's because she's not as qualified! If she gets paid less, it's because she didn't negotiate as well. And let me tell you something else:

(**SHEENA** *gives a sign to* **JODY** *and* **MARC**.)

SHEENA. *(cont.)* The WNBA is on the verge of bankruptcy, not because people are afraid to see women as strong and powerful, but because CHICK BASKETBALL IS BORING!

(**JODY** *and* **MARC** *spring on her.* **MARC** *grabs the drill as* **JODY** *tapes her mouth shut.*)

FRANCES. HEY! HEY –

(*as they get the tape over her mouth*)

MRWRUGH! HOMRWMIGITIZ!

MARC. Tie her hands up.

JODY. Hold her down!

(**JODY** *ties her hands.*)

MARC. Hurry. Just hold still! You're not going anywhere.

FRANCES. MURMIGURMITO!

JODY. There. That should hold for a little while.

(*They have finished the job.* **FRANCES** *sits in the wheelchair, hands bound, gagged with tape. She is seething, but for once, she is silent.* **MARC** *moves her out of the way.*)

MARC. We'll deal with her later.

SHEENA. I'm not stupid, Mother, I know what I'm doing.

JODY. All right. I'm gonna untie Madison and call the cops.

MARC. No.

JODY. What.

MARC. We're gonna keep going.

JODY. Dude –

MARC. We'll just let her calm down.

JODY. She wrestled me down on a bed of carpet tacks!

MARC. WE ARE FINISHING THE MOVIE.

Get Madison, and get reset for the shot.

(**JODY** *exits.*)

SHEENA. Marc, I am so sorry.

(MARC *goes to her, crouches down next to her, tenderly.*)

MARC. Are you okay?

SHEENA. I'm fine. I'm just embarrassed, all of this is happening because of me.

MARC. You don't have anything to be embarrassed about.

SHEENA. You really think we can leave her tied up there while we shoot?

(*They look at* FRANCES. *She tries to scream.*)

MARC. Yep.

SHEENA. When we get a break, I'll call her doctor.

MARC. All right. Now get ready to be impaled.

(JODY *enters with* MADISON, *her meat hook is ridiculously crushed, her costume comically askew.*)

JODY. Um, we've got a little bit of a problem.

MARC. Okay, okay, Amanda can fix this.

JODY. Dude –

MARC. AMANDA!

JODY. She left! she was a little traumatized, you know?

MARC. All right. All right, Madison, honey, you doing okay?

MADISON. Yeah, I guess –

MARC. Good.

(MARC *rips her hook off.*)

MADISON. Ow!

MARC. Here.

(MARC *takes the knife off his belt, swiftly cuts the straps off her tank top so she looks like she's wearing a tube top.*)

MADISON. (*as he cuts her straps*) Oh! Oh!

(*He gets a bottle of blood, squirts it on her.*)

MARC. Okay, what else?

(*He grabs a short, spiky wig.*)

Put this on!

(She puts the wig on. **MARC** *and* **JODY** *futz with her costume and hair for a second. They stand back and look at her.)*

MARC. What do you think?

JODY. You don't think anyone's going to recognize her from earlier?

MARC. She's gonna be a corpse in 15 seconds.

JODY. She looks great.

MARC. PLACES.

*(***JODY*** pulls on* **VICTOR***'s mask as they scramble to get into position.)*

MADISON. What are we doing?

JODY. I have no idea.

MADISON. Okay.

MARC. Madison, we'll start with you. VICTOR you're gonna drag her over, show her off to Sloan, and then kill her

JODY. Got it.

SHEENA. What about the scene where Victor tells Madison about Elise?

MARC. Nobody cares! Give me FEAR, give me TERROR, give me BLOOD. And no matter what happens, NO ONE STOPS.

Everybody ready?

(They nod.)

And....ACTION.

(Filming begins. Everyone tries to follow **MARC***'s directions.)*

*(***JODY/VICTOR*** holds* **MADISON** *around the neck, threatening her with a prop knife. She struggles to get away from him.)*

MADISON. *(in her movie voice)* "Get off me, let me go!"

*(***JODY/VICTOR*** drags her over in front of* **SHEENA/ SLOAN***.)*

MARC. Get her closer.

MADISON. "Help me, please, help me!"

MARC. Reach out to her, she's you're only hope, that's it.

SHEENA/SLOAN. "Just let her go!"

MARC. Do it!

(**JODY/VICTOR** *slices* **MADISON***'s neck, blood shoots out like a geyser.*)

MARC. And Madison: death shake!

(**MADISON** *shimmies her shoulders and chest.*)

SHEENA/SLOAN. "NO!"

MARC. Madison, keep reaching for Sloan, keep reaching, try to speak – and Victor drop her!

(**JODY/VICTOR** *drops* **MADISON** *with a thud.*)

MADISON. Ow!

JODY. Sorry.

MARC. Keep going. Move in on Sloan.

(**JODY/VICTOR** *moves toward* **SHEENA/SLOAN***. She tries to back away, but she's still handcuffed to the radiator.* **FRANCES** *watches intently.*)

SHEENA/SLOAN. "No, please, no –"

JODY/VICTOR. *(in his movie villain voice)* "Now it's just us."

SHEENA/VICTOR. "Please, just let me go!"

(*He shows off the prop knife.*)

JODY/VICTOR. "You're all mine."

SHEENA/SLOAN. "No, please!"

MARC. Smear some blood on her chest.

SHEENA. Um –

(**JODY** *and* **SHEENA** *both look at* **MARC***.* **JODY** *tentatively smears the blood on* **SHEENA***'s chest, being very careful to not touch her breasts.*)

JODY/VICTOR. "I can…do whatever I want."

MARC. Really rub it in.

(**JODY/VICTOR** *rubs more vigorously, but still in the "safe zone."*)

SHEENA/SLOAN. "Don't touch me!"

MARC. Now grab her by the hair.

JODY. *(totally breaking from his **VICTOR** character)* Um, what?

MARC. I said grab her!

SHEENA. You could grab my arm, and –

JODY. Like here?

MARC. Grab her hair and pull her up –

SHEENA. Just give us a second to figure this out –

MARC. Shut up and give me the mask!

SHEENA. What?

MARC. I said give me the mask!

JODY. Okay.

(**MARC** *takes the mask from* **JODY***, puts it on.*)

SHEENA. I'm sorry, what are we doing?

MARC. *(to **JODY**)* Just keep her in the frame.

JODY. Got it.

SHEENA. Marc –

MARC. And don't stop filming.

SHEENA. Wait, what are we doing?

MARC. Whatever we have to.

*(to **JODY**)*

Ready!

JODY. Action.   — Start

(**MARC/VICTOR** *moves in to* **SHEENA/SLOAN** *with the prop knife.* **SHEENA** *tries to resume acting, but as the threat of* **MARC***'s actions becomes more real, all artifice drops away.*)

SHEENA/SLOAN. "Please, no!"   — Cross [page]

MARC/VICTOR. Why didn't you listen to me?

SHEENA. "I should have –"

MARC/VICTOR. You should have stayed home with me instead of going off with that boy –

SHEENA. "I'm sorry!"

MARC/VICTOR. Liar! — *Pun up to my knees.*

    (**MARC/VICTOR** *grabs* **SHEENA**'s *hair on the top of her head and pulls her up to her knees by her hair.*)

SHEENA. Ow! You're hurting me!

MARC/VICTOR. Just like you hurt me.

    (**MARC/VICTOR** *cranks her head back so she is looking up at him, he caresses her face.*)

MARC. You were the only one who understood me –

SHEENA. Please –

MARC/VICTOR. Who believed in me –

SHEENA. You're really hurting me –

MARC/VICTOR. And you left!

    (*He gives her head another rough jerk.*)

SHEENA. (*screams*) Stop!

    (**MARC** *has completely strayed from the script.*)

MARC. You're so beautiful.

SHEENA. Stop it, just stop – — *Marc uncuff*

MARC/VICTOR. Everyone telling me no, telling me it's not right – *move away , Marc grab me*

SHEENA. Fucking let go of me! –

MARC/VICTOR. Telling me I wasn't good enough –

SHEENA. You're really hurting me –

JODY. Um, okay, maybe we should –

MARC/VICTOR. But not this time –

SHEENA. Stop the camera, stop!

MARC/VICTOR. I SAY WHEN WE STOP.

    (*He throws her down forcefully and straddles her, pinning her to the ground. He tosses the prop knife aside, takes out his knife from his belt.* **SHEENA** *is crying now.*)

SHEENA. No!

JODY. I don't think this is in the script – — *takes keys*

SHEENA. What are you doing?

MARC/VICTOR. I just needed something a little, sharper.

SHEENA. No, stop –

JODY. Maybe we should stop for second –

MARC/VICTOR. *(to* **JODY***)* KEEP FILMING.

> *(to* **SHEENA***)*

> Now you have to stay very still. I would hate for something bad to happen.

> *(***MARC** *runs the knife along* **SHEENA***'s neck.)*

SHEENA. Okay, okay, I'll be still.

MARC/VICTOR. That's my girl.

> *(He runs the knife between her breasts.)*

> First we have to get you out of these clothes.

SHEENA. No, stop, Marc – Jody? Stop!

MARC/VICTOR. *Just react.*

> *(He takes his knife, puts the point of it under the center of her bra, as though he's going to slice it open.* **FRANCES** *suddenly springs up from her chair. She has worked one of her hands free, and she runs, full-force, at* **MARC***. They wrestle.* **JODY** *jumps in and tries to pull them apart.* **FRANCES** *fights fiercely.)*

MADISON. *(whispers to* **SHEENA***)* Is this part of the movie?

SHEENA. No!

> *(***FRANCES** *knocks* **JODY** *out, turns her attention back to* **MARC***.* **MADISON** *slowly moves toward the door.)*

MARC. I've had enough of you!

> *(***MARC** *knocks* **FRANCES** *to the ground. He grabs her ankle, pulls her toward him.)*

MARC. Oh no you don't!

SHEENA. JUST STOP!

MADISON. Someone let me know about the call time for tomorrow, 'k?

MARC. Madison get back here!

> *(***FRANCES** *grabs the cordless drill and attacks* **MARC***.)*

MARC. *(to* FRANCES*)* What the fuck!

MADISON. Okay, see ya!

> (MADISON *exits.* MARC *and* FRANCES *struggle,*
> FRANCES *gets the drill very close to* MARC*'s face.)*

MARC. No no no no no no –

SHEENA. Leave her alone!

> (MARC *pushes* FRANCES *back. With his hands clasped*
> *over her own, he turns her hands so that the drill is now*
> *facing* FRANCES*. She tries to back away, but* MARC *is*
> *too strong. He pushes the drill dangerously close to her*
> *neck.)*

SHEENA. CALL THE POLICE!

MARC. What's the matter? Nothing to say now? I remember you! Screaming all over the news, trying to make it
sound like I was the villain! Well nobody listened then,
and nobody's gonna listen now, so just shut up!

> (JODY *is finally able to get up. He sees* MARC*, rushes*
> *over to help* FRANCES*, but stumbles into* MARC*, which*
> *sends the drill plunging into* FRANCES*' neck.)*

MARC. What…

No…

> (MARC *releases his hands,* FRANCES*' hands remain on*
> *the drill, which is still in her neck.* JODY *reaches over*
> *pulls it out of her.)*

JODY. Holy shit. We've gotta…

> (JODY *takes the tape out of her mouth. A puddle of blood*
> *begins to appear all around* FRANCES*' head and neck. It*
> *is dark, different from the movie blood.* FRANCES *makes*
> *terrible gurgling noises.)*

MARC. I was just holding it over her – I wasn't –

SHEENA. Oh my God –

JODY. Give me something to put on it.

MARC. I didn't –

SHEENA. What's happening?

(MARC hands him a t-shirt.)

JODY. Call an ambulance.

SHEENA. Is she okay?

JODY. Call them, now!

(MARC dials 911. JODY tapes the T-shirt to her neck with his gaff tape. The blood keeps coming.)

MARC. I need an ambulance, there's been an accident.

SHEENA. What's happening –

JODY. *(to FRANCES)* Just stay still, don't move. Holy shit, there's so much blood.

MARC. I think her neck is broken, she's bleeding –

SHEENA. SOMEBODY UNLOCK ME!

JODY. Oh my God, she's bleeding out.

SHEENA. SHE'S MY MOTHER! UNLOCK ME NOW!

(JODY rushes to SHEENA, fumbles for the key.)

MARC. 12695 Rancho Vista Way.

SHEENA. Oh my God, hang on, Mom. Just. I'm sorry, I'm sorry I said all those things the other night, I love you mom, I do. I just want to be happy, that's all! I don't want be angry at everybody all the time. I never meant to hurt you, please – WHAT THE HELL IS TAKING YOU SO LONG!

JODY. The key won't work!

(FRANCES looks at her watch. She sits, starts to stand. Blood has soaked through the T-shirt taped to FRANCES' neck and is pouring down her chest.)

MARC. Jesus Christ! She's getting up!

JODY. No, don't move – you'll lose more blood –

FRANCES. Shhhhhh, Sheena –

SHEENA. Mom?

(FRANCES is up, takes a few staggering steps towards SHEENA, who is still locked to the radiator. FRANCES tries to motion to SHEENA to get down.)

MARC. Ma'am, just sit back down –

SHEENA. Don't touch her!

FRANCES. Sh Sh Sh Sh Sh Sheena –

JODY. Please sit back down –

SHEENA. Mom, please! You're gonna die if you don't sit down, please please –

(With her last remaining strength, **FRANCES** *throws her body over* **SHEENA** *'s. A bright light flashes across the stage, along with the sound of a huge explosion.)*

(blackout)

(sound of sirens)

(A TV **NEWS ANCHOR** *appears in another area. She may be backed by video clips of* **SHEENA** *leaving a hospital in a wheel chair pushed by* **HILDY***, surrounded by flashing cameras.)*

NEWS ANCHOR. Authorities are still baffled by a bombing last week that left several people injured and one dead. Austin resident Frances McKinney was killed when a bomb was detonated at a residence in Round Rock. No body was recovered, but police say it would be impossible for anyone to have survived both the explosion and ensuing fire. The home was being used as a location for the upcoming horror movie, *Blood Bath.* In a movie worthy twist, police say the bomb was planted by McKinney, whose daughter, Sheena McKinney, stars in the forthcoming movie.

(Perhaps another video clip of **PASTOR DAN***, speaking at a podium, with* **CHRISTI GARCIA** *behind him, nodding in agreement.)*

Round Rock residents gathered last night for a prayer vigil to end violence organized by Holy Shepherd Church. Church leaders say they are planning to boycott the movie, but the movie's distributors don't appear to be worried. They've scheduled a press conference in town tomorrow, where they're expected to announce that film will be released in August. For WTEX Channel Five News, I'm Belinda Chapman.

Scene Eighteen

(Frances' house. **SHEENA** *enters wearing a short, low-cut black dress, her hair in a towel. She walks with a lumbering thud – one foot is in a cast, the other foot is bare.)*

SHEENA. I can't find my shoe.

HILDY. It's right here.

SHEENA. Not those, my black ones.

HILDY. The ones with the huge heels?

SHEENA. They're here somewhere –

HILDY. You can't wear those.

SHEENA. Watch me.

HILDY. You're not even supposed to be walking this much. The doctor said you're supposed to be taking it easy, not –

*(**SHEENA** has found the shoe and shoved her good foot into. She stands teetering a little.)*

SHEENA. *I am perfectly fine.*

(beat)

HILDY. Are you seriously wearing that to the press conference.

SHEENA. What's wrong with it?

HILDY. Nothing, for Shakira.

*(**SHEENA** takes off the shoe, carries it as she lumbers around the living room. She goes to the front door, opens it to look for the limo, leaves it open.)*

SHEENA. Well what else am I supposed to wear? I can't get pants on over my cast! This is the only other black I have!

HILDY. Oh, right! You're in mourning. I forgot, what with all the interviews, and your agent –

SHEENA. What is your problem?

HILDY. Nothing, why would I have a problem with you promoting a movie that our mother killed herself trying to stop –

SHEENA. You don't need to remind me what happened, I'm the one she was trying to blow up, remember?

HILDY. She saved your life!

SHEENA. Only at the last minute!

Only because she tried to kill me in the first place –

*(**SHEENA** starts to cry.)*

Crap.

HILDY. I'm sorry. I didn't mean to –.

You know you don't have to do this.

SHEENA. I'm doing it.

HILDY. They can still have their press conference without you, just –

SHEENA. *This is the biggest opportunity I'm ever gonna get. All right?* This is gonna pay off the house, pay for your college. That agent says he's got three movie offers for me already because of all the publicity. So if this is what I have to do to take care of both of us, that's what I'm gonna do.

(sound of a honk)

Crap. Tell them I'll be right there.

*(**SHEENA** lumbers off. **JODY** appears in the doorway. He wears a large neck stabilizing neck brace, and carries a cactus.)*

JODY. Hey.

HILDY. Hey.

SHEENA. *(offstage)* I just need two seconds!

HILDY. Hair.

JODY. Right.

I brought a cactus.

HILDY. Yeah.

JODY. Just to say, I'm sorry, for your loss.

(He gives it to **HILDY**.*)*

HILDY. Thanks.

JODY. You coming to the press conference?

HILDY. I take the PSAT tomorrow?

JODY. Oh.

HILDY. I think it's a little more important.

JODY. Definitely.

MARC. *(offstage)* Hildy!

HILDY. Plus someone has to look after Sheena's charity case.

JODY. Right.

> *(***MARC*** enters on* **FRANCES**' *scooter. He wears a bathrobe. He's got an awkward bandage over one eye and ear, and he's a little deaf from the blast.)*

MARC. *(to* **HILDY***)* The fridge is EMPTY. Don't you EAT anything in this house?

HILDY. I think we have pickles?

MARC. What?

HILDY. YOU WANT SOME PICKLES?

MARC. Jesus Christ, I want FOOD. What the hell is he doing here?

JODY. This is so weird.

> *(***SHEENA*** appears. Her hair is done.)*

SHEENA. Hey Jody.

JODY. Sheena. You look amazing.

SHEENA. Really?

JODY. Definitely.

MARC. What's going on?

SHEENA. He can't hear you, just ignore him.

JODY. For real?

MARC. Why are you so dressed up?

JODY. Look, Sheena, I'm really sorry, about your mom, and everything –

SHEENA. Thanks.

JODY. Things got so crazy at the end, and –

(*sound of another honk*)

SHEENA. It's okay. Let's do this.

MARC. You're doing something for the movie, aren't you?

JODY. He doesn't know about the press conference?

MARC. What are you doing, you're doing an interview?

SHEENA. Don't say anything.

MARC. HEY! Answer me!

SHEENA. (*loudly, so he can hear*) I am letting you stay here out of the kindness of my heart until your insurance settlement comes, but do not think for a second –

MARC. I wouldn't NEED to be here if YOUR MOTHER hadn't tried to BLOW US ALL UP!

SHEENA. (*to* **HILDY**) Will you be okay here?

MARC. Fine, go. We'll see who's the big star after my interview next week on Dateline NBC. Oh, they're very interested in my side of the story.

SHEENA. What are you talking about?

MARC. It seems you forgot to tell everyone how you got the part. How you came to my hotel room. Spent the night with me –

HILDY. What?

SHEENA. Nothing happened!

MARC. Oh, that's not how I remember it, Sheena.

SHEENA. (*to* **HILDY**) Hildy, get your stuff, you're coming with us.

HILDY. Good.

(**JODY** *helps* **HILDY** *gather her stuff.*)

MARC. They say you make it sound like a Lifetime movie. "Innocent co-ed trying to support her family gets exploited by evil director!" But nobody's gonna believe that when I'm done with you.

SHEENA. I'm through feeling sorry for you! I won't let you hurt me again.

(**SHEENA** *pulls out her phone, dials 911.*)

MARC. Hurt you? You got exactly what you wanted. Hell, you negotiated. You sold your tits and ass for fifteen grand.

(**SHEENA** *adjusts her dress, trying to make it more modest.*)

Look at you. You're still selling it. I think you'd better start learning Pilates.

SHEENA. *(on the phone)* Hi, there's an intruder in my house? He keeps saying he lives here.

(**SHEENA** *waves* **JODY** *and* **HILDY** *out the door.* **JODY** *stops, grabs the cactus for good measure, then exits.*)

MARC. You can't leave me here, HEY!

SHEENA. Yes, he's a white, male, about 40?

(*They are gone.* **MARC** *shouts after them.*)

MARC. You fuckers! Oh, fine, get in your limo! Live it up! We'll see who gets the last laugh!

(*He slams the door.*)

This is not over. This was MY movie, MY comeback. I'm gonna get on 60 Minutes. 48 Hours. *Doctor Phil.*

(*He zips back over to the door, to shout after them again.*)

I'll go to the National Fucking Inquirer –

(**MARC** *opens the door and sees:*)

(**FRANCES**. *She's covered in ash and dried blood, but she's strong and powerful. Lights shift.*)

(**MARC** *tries to back away, but his scooter won't work. She unsheathes a knife.*)

MARC. No. No no no no no –

FRANCES. *Oh yes.*

(**FRANCES** *raises the knife.*)

(*As* **MARC** *lets out a long girly scream: blackout.*)

End of Play

OTHER TITLES AVAILABLE FROM SAMUEL FRENCH

THAT PRETTY PRETTY; OR, THE RAPE PLAY

Sheila Callaghan

Comedy / 2m, 3f

A pair of radical feminist ex-strippers scour the country on a murderous rampage against right-wing pro-lifers, blogging about their exploits in gruesome detail. Meanwhile, a scruffy screenwriter named Owen tries to bang out his magnum opus in a hotel room as his best friend Rodney ("The Rod") holds forth on rape and other manly enterprises. When Owen decides to incorporate the strippers into his screenplay, the boundaries of reality begin to blur, and only a visit from Jane Fonda can help keep worlds from blowing apart.

Sheila Callaghan's *That Pretty Pretty; or, The Rape Play* is a violently funny and disturbing excavation of the dirty corners of our imaginations.

"Mind-blowing images and soul-crushing language flowing wildly."
–*Back Stage*

"A submersion in the anarchy of ambivalence: variously a rant, a riff, a rumble - about our notions of naturalism, objectification, perversity, and beauty ... There's sass and sarcasm in Callaghan's high-energy punk writing."
– *The New Yorker*

"Raunchy, savvy... the twisted, caffeinated world of the show imagines the collective subconscious of a culture where girls never stiop going wild... [Callaghan] push(es) her audience's buttons with an aggressive treatment of some of the darker corners of the human psyche."
–*The New York Times*

OTHER TITLES AVAILABLE FROM SAMUEL FRENCH

SCREAM QUEENS - THE MUSICAL

Scott Martin

Musical Comedy / 6f (ages 28 - 50+)

"They sing – they dance – they die!"

A hotel ballroom, 1998, and six voluptuous B-movie "Scream Queens" revive their fading acting careers by presenting a musical revue for their fans at a science fiction and horror film convention. From young newbie to seasoned grand dame, the Queens strut their stuff in song and dance to prove "I Got All of the Talent I Need." For 90 minutes of hilarious musical mayhem, they take the audience into the world of no-budget movies with awful scripts, fake monsters and gooey "Special FX." They even involve the audience in a screaming contest and zombie talent search.

As each Queen reveals her personal story, we share their hopes and dreams, from Tonya's love of her idol "Fay Wray" to Alexis' advice that "Everybody Starts at the Bottom" to DeeDee's secrets of Scream Queen longevity: "Don't Open That Door." British screen veteran Nadine savors her joy of being "Still In Demand" while Bianca celebrates the lifetime achievements of "Roger Corman" and Richelle laments her own elusive "Happy Endings." They also screen original clips from their direct-to-video "scary movie" spoofs such as "Revenge of the Psycho Bimbos" and "Malibu Vampire Vixens," all hoping to attract the attention of a popular young horror film director lurking in the audience.

The Scream Queens will have you convulsed with laughter and begging for the inevitable sequel.

"A sassy musical revue; an affectionate funny tribute…with something for everyone."
–*Los Angeles Times*

"Campy and full of shtick, affection and great fun!"
–*The Hollywood Reporter*

OTHER TITLES AVAILABLE FROM SAMUEL FRENCH

I USED TO WRITE ON WALLS

Bekah Brunstetter

Drama / 1m, 6f / Unit Set

Diane, Georgia and Joanne are 3 modern women living very different lives. Unbeknownst to them, they are all pining after the same young man, Trevor: sexy, stoned, oblivious; a surfer on a rad, rad philosophical journey. When a beautiful 11 year old girl named Anna, and Mona (a sexy, widowed astronaut) are thrown into the crosswinds of diverse romantic affairs, hearts will be broken, loves will be lost, and youthful cries of hope, anger, and sadness will be written on walls. Mothers will try to guide their daughters from the promise and beauty of youth through the diminishing opportunities of aging. Daughters will go to the extremes of passion to hold on to their fantasies of love. One man will be in the middle of a romantic storm of graffiti, drugs, sexual asphyxiation, gunshots, explosions, and desire.

OTHER TITLES AVAILABLE FROM SAMUEL FRENCH

TOMORROWLAND

Neena Beber

3m, 4f

Anna has left graduate school to join the real world, as a writer on a children's television show in Orlando, Florida, she finds that world to be more surreal and absurd than anything she's left behind. *Tomorrowland* takes a darkly comic look at death, Disney, and the search for meaning in a world that worships the young and the fake.

"Briskly hilarious comedy about a brittle New Yorker who abandons her doctoral dissertation on Virginia Woolf's use of parenthesis to write scripts for kid's TV show."
– Bob Mondello, *Washington City Paper*

"If you are not already terrified by the prospect of the Disneyfication of America, this wry exploration of its possible effects will put the fear of Mickey in you."
– Charlie Whitehead, *Time Out*

CPSIA information can be obtained at www.ICGtesting.com
Printed in the USA
BVOW06s0517140815

413003BV00008B/104/P